C.B. Coventry

Nature and Art in the Cure of Disease

Anatiposi

C.B. Coventry

Nature and Art in the Cure of Disease

Reprint of the original.

1st Edition 2023 | ISBN: 978-3-38230-090-6

Anatiposi Verlag is an imprint of Outlook Verlagsgesellschaft mbH.

Verlag (Publisher): Outlook Verlag GmbH, Zeilweg 44, 60439 Frankfurt, Deutschland
Vertretungsberechtigt (Authorized to represent): E. Roepke, Zeilweg 44, 60439 Frankfurt, Deutschland
Druck (Print): Books on Demand GmbH, In de Tarpen 42, 22848 Norderstedt, Deutschland

NATURE AND ART

IN THE

CURE OF DISEASE,

BY

C. B. COVENTRY, M. D.,

EMERITUS PROFESSOR OF PHYSIOLOGY AND MEDICAL JURISPRUDENCE IN
THE UNIVERSITY OF BUFFALO.

READ BEFORE THE

Medical Society of the County of Oneida, July, 1859.

PUBLISHED BY THE SOCIETY

UTICA:
ROBERTS, BOOK & JOB PRINTER, HERALD OFFICE, 60 GENESEE STREET
1859.

NATURE AND ART

IN THE

CURE OF DISEASE,

BY

C. B. COVENTRY, M. D..

EMERITUS PROFESSOR OF PHYSIOLOGY AND MEDICAL JURISPRUDENCE IN
THE UNIVERSITY OF BUFFALO.

———— • ◄●► • ————

READ BEFORE THE

Medical Society of the County of Oneida, July, 1859.

———— • ◄●► • ————

PUBLISHED BY THE SOCIETY.

———— • ◄●► • ————

UTICA:
ROBERTS, BOOK & JOB PRINTER, HERALD OFFICE, 60 GENESEE STREET.
1859.

PREFACE.

————•••————

THE following observations on Nature and Art in the Cure of Disease, have been elicited by the recent publication, in this country, of the work of Sir John Forbes, M.D., F.R.S., entitled, *Nature and Art in the Cure of Disease*, and a small work of Jacob Bigelow, M. D., of Boston, entitled, *Rational Medicine.* Though differing in title, the works are similar in sentiment and character ; and both unite in professing to expose what they consider the errors and faults of the profession to which the writers belong ; and both, though professedly addressed to the profession, are evidently intended for non-professional readers. Indeed, Dr. Forbes says, " One object has been to prepare a work which, while fulfilling its strictly professional aim, should also be calculated to convey to educated and instructed persons of all classes, such information respecting the real nature of disease, and the true character and power of the medical art, as they would be capable of comprehending and appreciating." Dr. Forbes admits that the doctrines promulgated in his work " are at variance with those entertained by many of our best informed medical men." It would have been supposed that a man who had long practiced, and enjoyed the honors and emoluments of the medical profession, would have hesitated in promulgating doctrines which he admits are at variance with the mass of the profession, and of many of its best informed members ; or would have, at least, been able to give some satisfactory reason for such a course. A very careful examination of the work of Dr. Forbes has not enabled the writer to discover the evidence that the Doctor is right or the profession wrong, or to justify him in terming the medical profession an " inert fraternity." It is believed that no intelligent and unbiassed person, out of the profession, can rise from the perusal of the work of Dr. Forbes without the conviction that it is a labored effort to destroy public confidence in the medical profession. And certainly no member of the profession can read either the works of Drs. Forbes or Bigelow without feelings of mortification and humiliation.

Believing that both writers are mistaken as to the actual practice of the profession, as well as to its actual benefits to the community ; and that the influence of both works is only evil to the community as well as to the profession ; the writer had hoped that some more able and influential pen than his own, would have exposed the sophisms and errors of the writers under consideration ; or that some of the numerous medical Journals and Reviews would have vindicated the character and honor of the profession. As yet, he has seen no such vindication. On the contrary, the notices which have met his eye, have been meager in the extreme, and a kind of half-endorsement of the works.

It was under these circumstances that the writer was induced to prepare and read the following remarks before the Medical Society of the County of Oneida, at its Annual Meeting in July, 1859. The Society, believing that the views presented were just, and that the honor of the profession would be promoted by giving them a more extended circulation and a more permanent form, kindly asked a copy for publication. The writer believes that thirty years' practice of his profession, a connection at different times with three different Medical Schools, and a pretty extensive consultation business in Central New York, enabled him to judge as to what is the practice of the intelligent portion of the profession in this country. Whether he is right, or the writers of the two works under consideration, is respectfully submitted to the medical profession to judge.

NATURE AND ART

IN THE

CURE OF DISEASE.

ALL practitioners of medicine of much experience in the treatment of disease, must have, often and painfully, felt how difficult it was at times to determine how far they should trust to the unaided recuperative powers of nature ; and when, and to what extent, they should endeavor to aid, or assist, or modify such efforts. All intelligent medical men admit and bow to the supremacy of the principle implanted in the constitution, which the older writers termed, the " *vis medicatrix natura*," and without which our science and art would be comparatively useless. It is believed that most practitioners will admit, that in all cases where some definite good or some precise object is not to be accomplished by the administration of medicine, it is better to abstain from its use, and trust the cure to nature, aided by such regulations of diet, air and exercise, as the experience of the medical profession, and of the individual practitioner, may direct. Such was the doctrine which I was taught, and the correctness of which has been confirmed by thirty years' experience in the practice of our profession. Such we believed to be the established practice of the profession at the present time. It is true that I have heard of a practitioner in former times, who, when asked the object of a prescription containing numerous ingredients, some of which were chemically and others medically incompatible, replied, " If you give a little of every thing, something will hit the mark." I trust no such practitioner, claiming to be of the profession, can be found at the present day.

It is a common and vulgar error to suppose that the whole of the practice of medicine consists in the administration of medicine. No less skill and experience is required to direct the hygiene treatment, the regulation of the diet, rest, exercise, bathing and fresh air, and to determine when and to what extent medicine is necessary, than to direct what medicine should be given.

Many diseases require no medicine ; a removal of the cause, rest and abstinence is all that is required. Many others, no doubt, if left to themselves, would in time subside, without any aid from medicine. It is, however, equally certain that the timely interference of art in the early stage of a disease, will often check and arrest its progress, or convert into a mild, what would have otherwise been a severe if not fatal disease.

Many diseases, particularly the exanthemata, run a specific course, and may be considered self-limited ; too active or perturbating treatment, adopted with the view of arresting or breaking up the disease, may do more harm than good. As much skill is necessary in a pilot to manage his vessel safely through a storm, when no harbor is nigh, as to run her safely into port when that is possible. The wind may be trusted to propel a vessel, but a skillful pilot is necessary to direct her course. So, just as much experience and skill is necessary to conduct a patient safely through a self-limited disease, as to arrest or cut short a disease where this is possible. Even in those fatal diseases, where both nature and art are powerless to save the patient from death, an intelligent and conscientious physician can do much to sooth the suffering of his patient, and smooth the road, though he knows it must lead to the grave. It is a peculiarity in the human constitution, and one to which Americans are said to be particularly prone, to run into extremes. It is not improbable that the profession, as well as the public, may formerly have run into the extreme of placing too much reliance on art, or the administration of medicine, in disease, and too little on the unaided efforts of Nature. When we look at our papers, and see column after column filled by advertisements of pretended specifics for every imaginable form of disease, it is a certain evidence of the credulity of the community as to the influence and power of medicine in curing disease, and a foreshadowing of what is sure to follow (and what is even now beginning to manifest itself), viz., a distrust in the medical profession, and in the use of all medicine. It is but a short time since a distinguished lecturer and divine,*

* Henry Ward Beecher.

made the declaration, in a public lecture, that all that the doctors did was to coax their patients to cure themselves. This was about as rational as to assert that all the surgeon did was to coax his patients to dress their own fractured limbs, or restore their dislocated joints. That the mass of the people, when they find from sad experience, how false and fallacious are the promises made in the quack advertisements in the papers, should loose their confidence in medicine, is perfectly natural ; but that educated and intelligent men should argue against the medical profession, because charlatans and unprincipled individuals have made it a cloak for practicing on the ignorance and credulity of the community, is surpassing strange. No class in the community have so perseveringly and unremittingly protested against this fraud and imposition, as the medical profession ; and for the best of reasons, because no other body of men could see or know so well the evils it was inflicting on a credulous community. Medicines are only useful when adapted to the particular stage of the disease, and the actual condition of the patient. Every intelligent practitioner knows that the idea of any particular article of medicine being adapted to all or different diseases, to the different stages of the same disease, or to different constitutions, or to different conditions of the system, is an absurdity. It would be as reasonable to hold the Christian religion and its ministers responsible for all the crimes and cruelties committed in the name and under the cloak of religion, as to hold the medical profession responsible for the sins and errors of empiricism. The delusion of Homeopathy is gradually dying out. Already most of its professed advocates have abandoned the doctrine of infinitesimal doses, which constituted its only peculiarity. Credulity, in medicine as in other matters, is apt to be followed by scepticism, and those who but a short time since were ready to attribute miraculous powers to little pellets of sugar, are now ready to denounce all medicine and the medical profession.

Under these circumstances, it becomes a question of serious import, for the profession to determine what course to pursue. Shall they continue to claim for their profession the high and dignified position which has been accorded to it in every civilized community, and to which the character of the great body of its members should entitle it, or quietly submit to the taunts of Dr. B., and the thousands who represent the profession as simply coaxing the patient to cure himself, or join those who, after partaking of the honors and profits of the profession, turn round and abuse it ; or to represent, with Dr. Forbes, that all the physician does is to amuse the patient whilst nature cures the disease, but that the physician too often interferes with the kind provisions of nature, thwarts her salutary efforts, and injures rather than benefits his patient.

In one sense, it is true that a physician has no power to cure disease. All that he can do is to place his patient, as far as possible, in that condition in which the ordinary laws of nature will effect a restoration. Art is but the minister and handmaid of Nature, fulfilling those conditions which are necessary to enable Nature to act with success. Thus the agriculturist, when he prepares his soil with care, selects his seed and deposits it in the earth, at a time when the warmth of the sun and timely showers, tends to promote vegetation, only fulfills the necessary conditions imposed by the laws of nature. But this is not all ; he knows that the young plant must be supplied with nourishment, in the form of manure, and that the weeds must be extirpated. He knows that he has no power to make a single seed to vegetate, but he also knows that nature never supplies the want of knowledge and care on his part. The surgeon has no power to unite a fractured limb ; he can only place the parts in coaptation, keep them quiet, and trust to nature to effect a union. So in the practice of medicine. Art has no power to cure disease ; it can only aid, as in agriculture, in fulfilling the conditions under which Nature acts. In some cases, Art can remove the cause of disease. In some, when the cause cannot be removed, it can neutralize or modify its virulence. In some, it may supply the means or agencies which Nature requires to effect her purpose. To speak, then, of the powers of Art as compared with Nature in the cure of disease, is simply an absurdity. The true question is, How far can Art assist Nature in the cure of disease? When we reflect on the amount and variety of knowledge required for this purpose, humble as it may appear, and the noble and benevolent purposes for which it is acquired, it will detract nothing from the honor or dignity of the medical profession.

Lest I should be charged with misrepresentation, I prefer to let the authors to whom I have referred, speak for themselves. Dr. Bigelow says,—" I sincerely believe that the unbiased opinion of most medical men of sound judgment and long experience, is made up, that the amount of disease and death in the world would be less, if all disease were left to itself, than it now is, under the multifarious, reckless and contradictory modes of practice, good and bad, with which practitioners of adverse denominations carry on their differences at the expense of their patients."*

If the Doctor, by the term practitioners, means the regular profession of medicine, I think you will agree with me in pronouncing it a libel on the profession. If he means to embrace every species of empirical practice, and the use of the numerous nostrums, the advertisement of which disgrace our papers, why introduce it here ? or, why leave it to be inferred that he is speaking of the medical profession ? The Profession of Medicine is certainly not responsible for it, for no body of men have labored so hard to suppress it. But even admitting all the evils of quackery and empiricism, there is one simple fact, which is a complete answer to the doctor's supposition ; and that is, that the value of life has nearly if not quite doubled during the last one hundred years, and that this amelioration was mainly effected through the instrumentality of the medical profession.

Dr. Bigelow says, " The cumbrous fabric now called Therapeutic science, is in a great measure built up on the imperfect testimony of credulous, hasty, prejudiced and incompetent witnesses : such as have afforded authorities for books like Murray's *Apparatus Medicamentum* and Hahnemann's *Organon."* " The cumbrous polypharmacy of modern times, is an excrescence on science, unsupported by any evidence of necessity or fitness ; and of which the more complicated formulas are so arbitrary and useless, that if by any chance they should be forgotten, not one in a hundred of them would ever be reinvented." Here, again, the Doctor leaves it to be inferred that he is speaking of the medical profession, or of medical science ; and yet, by his speaking of the *Organon,* we must suppose that he refers to the multifarious systems of empiricism, which are only excrescences on medical science. Dr. B. says, " To prescribe blindly for symptoms irrespectively of their cause, is often in the highest degree

* Exposition of Rational Medicine, page 41.

B

injudicious."* Every intelligent physician admits this, as it in fact constitutes the true distinction between the empiric and the educated and intelligent physician. As far as can be judged from the Doctor's book, he seems to make no distinction between the regular profession of medicine, and the hosts of empiricism, which has always been its worst enemies; thus he places Dr. Rush and Brandreth in the same category.

Dr. Forbes starts with the proposition that the great defect in the medical profession is a want of a natural history of disease. He says, " In a very early stage of my medical experience, I became impressed with the conviction that the most fruitful source of false views, both in pathology and practice in the profession originated in ignorance of the natural laws that govern disease ; in other words, in ignorance of the *natural history of disease.*"

Whilst the Doctor admits that there has been some improvement in certain departments of medicine, he says, as to this particular department, " Infinitely less progress has been made, insomuch that it may be affirmed that the practitioners of the present day are, speaking generally, almost as uninformed in this particular, as were their predecessors fifty or a hundred years back."

Speaking of the object of the work, Dr. F. says, " Its main purpose is to prove the immense power possessed by Nature to cure disease of her own autocracy, and without any aid from Art." Dr. F. adds, " Such has ever been the want of trust in Nature, and the over-trust in Art, prevalent among members of the medical profession, that the field of natural observation has been to a great extent hidden actually from their eyes, or virtually from their apprehension. The constant interference of Art, in the form of medical treatment, with the normal process of disease, has not only had the frequent effect of distorting them in reality, but even when it failed to do so, has created a belief that it did so ; leading, in either case, to an inference equally wrong ; the false picture in one instance supposed to be true, the true picture in the other supposed to be false." " With these impressions on their minds, it was scarcely possible for the practitioner not to form a false estimate alike of the power of Nature and of the power of Art in modifying and curing disease ; underrating the former in the same proportion as they exaggerated the latter ;

* Exposition of Rational Medicine, p. 55.

and the consequence has been, that diseases have been treated mainly as if Nature had little or nothing to do in their cure, and Art almost every thing." In this country, we do not labor under the same difficulty as Dr. Forbes, for whilst cases are not unfrequent where absolutely nothing is done in the way of medication, we are frequently called to cases which are equivalent, where the period is permitted to pass, in which treatment could be of any possible use, before a physician is called ; so that ample opportunity is given to learn the natural history of the disease, and what the result when unaided by Art.

Dr. Forbes says, " If it be true, as I believe, that the doctrine respecting the power of Nature to cure disease, promulgated in the present work, are at variance as regards degree, with those entertained by many of our best informed and most experienced medical men, and at variance in every respect and in an extreme degree, with those entertained by a majority of our junior and ordinary practitioners, it seems requisite that the grounds of so important a difference should be stated."*

" Since the Medical Art assumed its present formal, bold and complicated character, it is only in rare and exceptional cases that the disease is left to Nature or treated regimenally. On the contrary, the strongest and most effective powers of Art are usually employed, for the purpose of counteracting or modifying in some way or other, the powers of Nature. Generally speaking, we may say that all the heroic arms of physic are invoked purposely to disturb, and obstruct, and overwhelm the normal process."†

Of course, I would not question the truth of Dr. Forbes' statement as applied to his own country and his own experience. I can only say, it is directly at variance with the doctrines which I was taught ; with the practice of the intelligent portion of the profession in this country, so far as my knowledge extends ; and with the doctrines taught in most, if not all our medical schools.

Dr. Forbes says, " The most zealous advocates of the dignity of the medical art, must admit, that if it is not altogether conjectural, many of its most important conclusions must be allowed to rest on no better foundation than the balance of probabilities."‡

The Doctor, however, discovers that we have the means of

---

* Nature and Art in Disease, p. 24.   † Ib., page 33.   ‡ Ib., page 46.

testing the natural history of disease, 1, By its results in savage and uncivilized nations, where they depend on charms and incantations, and where they give no medicines internally ; 2, The results of Homeopathic practice, which he considers equivalent to giving no medicine, and the results of disease in animals. I shall not stop to question the propriety or consistency of drawing inferences from the diseases of animals, or from persons in a savage state of society, where the modes of living and habits are so different from civilized life ; but shall examine, very briefly, his second proposition, viz., the evidence drawn from Homeopathy.

Dr. F. says, " The *saphias* or charms used by the Africans are equally efficacious. One popular form of these, mentioned and described by Mungo Park, consists in writing the charm on a board, and drinking the matter of the words, when it has been carefully washed off. A mode of practice very analogous to, and we doubt not as efficacious, as that of the Homeopathists, who, in point of fact, if they adhere rigidly to the original Hahnemannic doses, do literally prescribe words and not things."*

Speaking of Homeopathy, Dr. F. says, " It can be demonstrated that the treatment legitimately derived from it, of prescribing infinitesimals, in other words, imaginary doses of drugs, is entirely incapable of modifying the animal organism, in any way except through the medium of the patient's mind, or by means of dietetics and other regimenal means, with which the treatment may be combined."† Inert as he considers these means, he thinks them as successful as the regular practice of the profession, or rather professes so to think. He says, " And yet, what is the character of the results obtained under this system of imaginary medication in the cure of disease ? When fairly weighed, do not these results exhibit, if not quite as large a proportion of cures as ordinary medicine, still so large a proportion as to demonstrate at once the feebleness of what we regard as the best form of Art, and the immense strength of Nature in the same office."‡

Dr. Forbes adds, " It is unnecessary in this place to adduce any fresh proofs of the truth of the opinion here assumed, that Homeopathic remedies, so called, are utterly inert and incapable of influencing the body in any of its organs or functions, whether

* Nature and Art in Disease, p. 145.   † Ib., page 159.   ‡ Ib., page 160.

in health or disease. This, to me, is a demonstrated fact, and must remain a demonstrable fact so long as Homeopathy adheres to the doctrine and practice of its founder in regard to infinitesimal doses. It is, then, in the system of Homeopathy alone that we can find an example of expectation in its perfectly pure state, as it is only in the practice of its followers that we can find an entire abstinence from all drugs of possible power. It is, therefore, from this source that we must draw our conclusions respecting the value of pure *Expectation* as a form of therapeutics, which, it need hardly be remarked, is precisely the same as drawing conclusions respecting the power of Nature in curing disease. I know not if Homeopathy, whilst rejecting all rational medical treatment, is inconsistent enough to sanction and adopt the regimenal practice of ordinary medicine. If so, we must go further in our estimate, that it may be beneficial as well as innocent, inasmuch as it may positively aid Nature to the extent of the power of this foreign auxiliary." " To those who have assented to the principles propounded and the conclusions arrived at in the preceding parts of this work, such an estimate of its value will not appear a very low one, when compared with several of the modes of practice followed under the ordinary system." Not satisfied with the degradation of the regular profession, below Homeopathy, which he considers absurd and worthless, he adds, " But I will venture to go still further in the attempt to restrict the power, or rather, to define the real power of the medical Art, without any apprehension of thereby degrading it. Not only in the pestilential epidemics referred to, but even in the milder zymotic fevers, in the acute viceral inflammation, and in several forms of acute disease of a severe kind, the power of the Medical Art to positively save life, appears to be very circumscribed." Dr. F. says, " It is melancholy to be forced to make admissions in favor of a system so utterly false and despicable as Homeopathy, and in derogation of one which is both true and rational."*

It seems difficult to conceive what could have been the motive for publishing such a work. The Doctor disclaims any intention of degrading the medical profession ; at the same time, the most labored effort of an open opponent would have less effect in so doing. He says, " It is as an old member of this *inert fraternity*,

---

* Nature and Art in Disease, p. 248.

and as an expositor of doctrines sanctioned by their opinions and practice, that I have ventured to take upon myself my present task."* If the propositions of Dr. F. were indeed true, it would be a matter of humiliation and mortification to every honorable member of the profession, instead of the arrogant and exulting manner in which the work of Dr. F. is written. Fortunately for the credit of the medical profession, there is but little difficulty in exposing the sophisms and errors of the Doctor's statement. Thus, in every instance where the subject has been fairly tested, the vast superiority of the regular practice over Homeopathy has been demonstrated. A single instance, taken from the testimony given on a recent trial in France, will be sufficient. Dr. Charge, a Homeopathic physician of Marseilles, France, boasted that out of eighty (80) cases of cholera, he had not lost a single patient. When the disease broke out in 1856, the mayor of the city called on Dr. C., and delivered up to him one of the wards of the Hotel Dieu, a hospital of Marseilles, where every thing was arranged according to his desire. Dr. C., who had boasted of having never lost a cholera patient, lost, in eight days, twenty-one patients out of twenty-six, whilst in the adjoining ward, the regular practitioner lost but fourteen out of twenty-five patients.† Dr. Forbes thinks we have a powerful argument in favor of the admission that an average amount of recovery takes place under Homeopathic treatment, in the fact that no public outcry has been raised against it on the score of inefficiency, and yet more of mortality. The facts, however, are equally unfortunate for the Doctor's argument. It is notorious, that, notwithstanding the fact that many of the professed Homeopathists do resort to active treatment, and that a large proportion of the unfortunate and fatal cases pass into the hands of the regular practitioner when too late to be benefited,—that Homeopathy has seldom or never obtained a permanent footing in this country, where alone an opportunity is afforded of comparing and testing the result.

Both Drs. Forbes and Bigelow are unfortunate in enumerating cholera among the diseases that are not amenable to treatment. It is a fact well established, and for the correctness of which I

* Nature and Art in Disease, page 167.
† Boston Medical Journal, Vol. XL., No. 10, p. 195.

can vouch from ample personal experience, that the disease can—
in its first stage—with almost certainty, be arrested by medical
treatment. The Sanatory Commission of Great Britain were so
well satisfied of this fact, that they recommended the establish-
ment of Dispensaries, where those laboring under diarrhea—*i. e.*
the first stage of cholera—could apply.

The Editor of the *Medico-Chirurgical Review*, says, " There can
be no doubt of the existence of a premonitory stage in many
cases. It is well described by Annesly, and others since his
time ; and it is also certain that it can be often and at once arrested."* It is no argument against these facts, to say that in
the stage of collapse—when medicines are no longer absorbed—
they are powerless to cure the disease. Were I to select a case
going to show the powers of Art in successfully aiding and modifying the efforts of Nature in the cure of disease, it would be the
cholera. It is not our design to discuss the merits or demerits of
Homeopathy. If Dr. Forbes is correct in his supposition that it
is equally successful as the regular practice, it accomplishes what
was no doubt intended by its author, viz., to substitute an innocent and harmless delusion, for one which was less pleasant and
might be injurious. Our object has been to notice some of the
mistakes, not to say misrepresentations, of the works under consideration, and to show what is believed to be their natural and
legitimate effect on the profession and the community. The position professedly advocated by both Drs. Forbes and Bigelow,
that medicine should not be administered without clear and dis-
tinct views as to the nature of the disease, and the actual patho-
logical condition, and the effect proposed to be produced by the
medicinal agent, is no doubt correct ; it is precisely the course
adopted by every intelligent and well educated physician. What
we object to in both works is, what we believe to be a misrepresentation of the doctrine and practice of the regular profession,
and in confounding it with the hosts of empiricism ; pointing out
no distinction, and thus calculated to destroy public confidence
in the whole profession, and produce the very evil which Dr.
Bigelow professes to depricate, viz., " to lower the standard of
professional character, and raise empiricism to the level of honest
and enlightened physicians,"—or rather, in public estimation, to
reduce the enlightened and educated physician to the level of the

* Medico-Chirurgical Review, July, 1848, p. 106.

16

empiric. It is believed that Dr. Forbes places far too low an estimate on the exertions and influence of the profession in investigating the causes and preventives of disease. It is true that the great mass of the profession are actively engaged in practice, and have but little time for investigation ; but many of the ablest minds in the profession are devoted to such investigations, and every intelligent practitioner, in his own limited sphere, acts as a missionary to promulgate the truths they may discover.

We believe, too, that both Dr. Forbes and Dr. Bigelow have too little confidence in the use of medicine. Violent diseases sometimes require active treatment. Medical men, who are familiar with the malignant diseases of our Southern and Western States, would smile at the recommendations of Drs. Forbes and Bigelow. It is another instance, showing how absurd it is for men accustomed only to the diseases of London and Boston, to judge of what is necessary in the new settlements of our country. Homeopathy has never obtained a foothold in such localities. In the language of a very intelligent practitioner from a Southern city, "The climate is not congenial to it." It is very certain that a practitioner who adopted the do-nothing practice, would soon have nothing to do. This principle is well illustrated in the experience of your former associate, Dr. Alex. Coventry, who found that the lessons he had learned in the schools and lecture rooms of Scotland, would not answer in the backwoods of America. The older members of the Society, who were familiar with the practice of Dr. C., know how sparing and cautious he was in the use of medicine ; and yet he found from his experience in his own family and in his own person, that it was sometimes necessary to resort to active—what Dr. B. might stigmatize as heroic—treatment.*

* Dr. Coventry says, "Had I remained in the country of my birth and education; nay, had my location continued on the well cultivated banks of the North river, I should have probably to this day adhered to the doctrines I had imbibed from the venerable Cullen, and pursued the plan of practice taught by the admirable Gregory, But it was my destiny to pass another ordeal ; to verify the observation that one-half of life is spent in unlearning what was taught in the other half. I soon found that nosological arrangements, however applicable in the mild climate of Europe, in the healthy countries of England and France, availed but little among the swamps and marshes of the New World ; for there I often found fever assuming such protean features, such varying appearances, that before the ink was dry with which you had placed it in a class and order, a new symptom would arise, calling on you to alter its nomenclature."

We cannot conceal from ourselves the fact, that medicine as a profession has a very different position in the public estimation, from what it formerly had. Though often the subject of satire and ridicule, medicine, by the mass of the community, was looked upon with respect, amounting almost to veneration. The family physician was an oracle as to all that concerned the health of his employers. This relation is in a great measure abolished. Physicians and surgeons are employed as a mechanic or laborer, depending much upon locality or caprice. One man is employed to-day, another may be employed to-morrow. It is not unfrequent that one member of a family will employ one physician, and another member another ; so that often two, sometimes three, different medical men are in attendance on different members of the family at the same time. It cannot be denied that medicine as a science and an art has continued to improve in an equal ratio with the other sciences, and that physicians of the present day are better qualified to treat disease, and more entitled to public confidence, than their predecessors a century since. It is notorious that as a profession they possess much less of the public confidence, and that what exists, is confidence in the individual rather than in the profession. This is, no doubt, the necessary consequence, to a certain extent, of the existing law regulating the practice of medicine. Every man is at liberty to practice medicine, and to attach M. D. to his name ; and the kind public complacently dubs them all Doctors. The community generally know nothing, and care as little, for any distinction ; they form their opinion of the profession from their knowledge of those who are styled Doctors. Judged by this standard, I am free to confess that it is scarcely possible to form too low an opinion. As the legitimate practice of the profession, by a well educated, intelligent and honest practitioner, is one of the most noble and honorable occupations in which a man can engage ; so, on the other hand, for a man without medical education, for the mere sake of gain, to pretend to a knowledge of that of which he knows himself to be ignorant, and thus trifles with the health and lives of his fellow-men, is one of the most dishonorable and contemptible. Our papers often contain accounts of crimes and outrages committed by Dr. so and so ; though it is not contended that medical men are more free from crime than other professions, it is notorious that in a very large proportion of such cases, it will

C

be found, on investigation, to be persons who had no legitimate claim to the title of doctor, but had assumed it for some sinister purpose. Another cause which has contributed materially to destroy confidence in the medical profession, is that within the last few years, men who have been educated, and practiced the profession for years, have come out and denounced it. This embraces a large proportion of those who have gone over from the regular profession to embrace Homeopathy. They quiet their conscience —when they have any—by the argument, that the people will have a Homeopathic physician, that it will not lessen or destroy their capacity to practice medicine, and if they refuse to gratify them, they may fall into the hands of some one more ignorant than themselves. They seem to forget that a man is morally responsible, not only for the intention with which an act is committed, but for the influence which it is calculated to produce. If it is for the interest and good of society to have an intelligent and educated medical profession, then every encouragement to empiricism, every act which has a tendency to break down or destroy confidence in the profession, is inflicting a positive injury on the community. It was not, therefore, without reason that the Rev. Dr. Kennedy, in an address before the Albany Medical College, June, 1858, made the following remarks: "For myself, I believe I would suffer long and painfully, under the care of an intelligent and educated physician, before I would consent to receive a certain cure at the hands of an empiric ; for admitting by accident he cured me, yet by giving him my influence, he might have the opportunity of killing others, and I would be partaker of his sin." A highly intelligent and influential member of the legal profession, who gave the weight of his example and precept in support of Homeopathy, once told me that his medical attendant, though a professed Homeopath, was an educated physician, and he had confidence enough in his capacity and honesty, to believe he would do what was for the best. Admitting that he was correct in his estimate, of which I have strong doubts, he seemed entirely to overlook the deep moral responsibility he assumed in lending his influence in support of Homeopathy, at the expense of the regular profession. Another cause, which has no little influence in lessening public confidence in the medical profession and the use of medicine, is the promises held out, and the numerous certificates of cures published in the advertising columns of our papers. Every person of common sense knows how totally un-reliable are such promises and statements; and yet, there are thousands who, because they have been cheated by an advertising charlatan, denounce the doctors and the whole professson of medi-cine. That these causes should operate with the ignorant, is not surprising; but that intelligent and educated men should condemn the profession because our law-makers have unwisely encouraged the dishonest and unprincipled charlatan, to use it as a cloak for practicing on the credulity of the community, is strange.*

It becomes a serious question to inquire what is to be the effect of this state of things, on the profession and the community. As to the ultimate effect there can be no doubt, if it continues, viz., that of deterioration in the profession. All incentive to a noble ambition is destroyed. Young men of the proper qualifications will be loath to enter a profession, where success in business, and where public honor and distinction, depend less upon a knowl-edge of their profession, and upon a faithful discharge of its duties, than upon management, chicanery and intrigue. Where, in short, he must compete for public favor with the charlatan. With a firm reliance, however, on the ultimate good sense of the community, we believe that the medical profession will not only come out of the present ordeal unscathed, but more securely seated in the confidence and affections of the community.

Quackery will no doubt continue, as it always has continued, to exist. In every community, there are always a certain portion who are governed more by their love of the marvellous and in-comprehensible, than the stern dictates of their reason; but to suppose the mass of the community would not learn that medicine is no exception to the ordinary rules of reason, would be to ques-tion their capacity for self-government, or to judge what is for their own interest.

That the man who has faithfully devoted many years to the in-vestigation of the laws of health and disease, is better qualified to judge and direct in those subjects, than one of equal capacity

* Within the last few years many efforts have been made, by the organization of the American Medical Association, and by the State Medical Societies, to elevate the medical profession, and the standard of medical education; but all such efforts must prove vain, unless some mode can be adopted to draw a line of demarcation between the educated physician and those who only assume the title from some selfish or sinister motive.

who has had no such training, does not admit of a doubt. " In all cases, in the worst, there is one course more prudent than another. If the ship is running on the shore, or is even breaking up on the rocks, there may be one course better than another in the management of affairs. In the worst peril, in which you must leave the bark to which you have trusted yourself, in whose guidance would you place most confidence ? Would you leave yourself to the mercy of the waves ? Would you trust an ordinary sailor, because he bawled the loudest ? or would you follow the advice of the experienced shipmaster ?"* A physician is simply a student of nature, and as such, the whole of nature is open to his investigation. If he has conformed to the requirements of the law, and given satisfactory evidence of his capacity to judge, he is not only at liberty, but is bound to adopt any course of practice which he conscientiously believes best for his patient. If he believes vegetable medicine preferable to minerals, he uses them. If he believes cold bathing would be useful, he adopts it. To say that a man is a Botanic doctor, a Hydropath, or a Homeopath, is simply to say that he restricts himself to one particular department of Nature, instead of availing himself of the whole. If a regular practitioner abandons the regular profession, to adopt the insignia of a particular clique, as Botanic doctor, Hydropath, or Homeopath, we may justly question the motive, for he voluntarily —if he is honest in his change—deprives himself of some of the most important resources of his art, and gets in return simply a new name. To suppose that such name could add anything to his capacity to treat disease, would be an absurdity.

Prof. Ware, of Boston, in an eloquent discourse, alludes to the subject under consideration in the following terms :—

" The following considerations, I cannot but think, have much weight in enabling us to judge of the probable future and destiny of our profession ; namely, that whatever may be the currency of particular opinions, or the reputation of particular bodies of practitioners, the public will confide habitually and mainly in that body or that succession of men, who show themselves to be devoted to medicine, not merely as a means of getting a livelihood, or even as a means of treating disease and relieving suffering by the common routine practice ; but who pursue it as a great

* Letters to a Young Physician, by James Jackson, M. D., LL. D., &c.

subject, all the relations and bearings of which it is their duty to investigate ; who regard it as a science they are deputed to build up and perfect ; and who do all as diligent and disinterested inquirers after truth. It is this class of men who, when they are understood, will receive the permanent confidence of mankind ; and such, I undertake to assert, has been, and is, the essential character of our profession."*

Dr. Ware refers not only to the self-sacrificing devotion of medical men in the practice of their profession, but to their contributions to the collateral sciences. He says, " These services of the medical profession, upon the whole, have been among the most disinterested ever rendered to mankind. They have been distinctly governed by a desire of acquiring that knowledge which will confer practical benefits on society, without reference to the amount of reward, or to any fame except that of doing good. There is no better proof of this than the fact already implied, that the aim of those who are most prominent in medical history, has been more to investigate the laws of disease, and then prevent it, and raise the standard of health, than to acquire reputation and wealth by what is far easier and more lucrative—attention to the ordinary details of medical practice. And if it were necessary to introduce a more striking example of what is to be regarded as the governing spirit of those who are the true index of professional character, we have but to name the discovery and gift of vaccination to mankind by the illustrious Jenner."† It is, however, admitted that there are members of the profession who are actuated by less lofty motives. He says, " To them, the practice of medicine is like the practice of any other occupation, selected and followed almost mechanically. Hence, there are always to be found physicians of sordid minds and purely selfish views, who are yet high in professional rank and emolument. Such men, naturally enough—but unfortunately for our good name—have often been the most prominent to the public eye, and have been the chief recipients of public favor and patronage, just as it happens in all other departments ; and they have been thus sometimes taken as exponents of the character of the profession. But its true representatives are those to whose lives and labors I

* Discourse on Medical Education, &c., by John Ware, M. D., Boston, p. 23.
† Ib. page 23.

have just referred ; and from these men the treasures of knowledge, which they have accumulated in years of faithful and unceasing labor, has descended to us as our rich inheritance, possessed of which we should feel safe as to our future destiny. Whatever may be the accidental and temporary alienation of portions of that public which we serve, and whose confidence is so necessary to our usefulness, if we are faithful to the true character of our profession, if we go forward in honest fidelity in the path of our predecessors, governed by the same desire of knowledge and of usefulness, we need not fear but that the present movement of opinion will be transient, and that our position will become more durable than before."*

* Discourse on Medical Education, by John Ware, M. D., p. 23.